GRAMPS,
I've Got a Problem

GRAMPS,
I've Got a Problem

Solve life's puzzles

RICHARD PALMQUIST

Copyright © Richard Palmquist.

All rights reserved. No part of this book may be reproduced in any form or by any electronic or mechanical means, including information storage and retrieval systems, without permission in writing from the publisher, except by reviewers, who may quote brief passages in a review.

ISBN: 978-1-64871-691-1   (Paperback Edition)
ISBN: 978-1-64871-692-8   (Hardcover Edition)
ISBN: 978-1-64871-690-4   (E-book Edition)

Some characters and events in this book are fictitious. Any similarity to real persons, living or dead, is coincidental and not intended by the author.

Book Ordering Information

Phone Number: 347-901-4929 or 347-901-4920
Email: info@globalsummithouse.com
Global Summit House
www.globalsummithouse.com

Printed in the United States of America

Contents

His Grandson Needs Help xi

Chapter 1 – We all have problems 1
Chapter 2 – A simple tool 4
Chapter 3 – One{three} fits everything everywhere 9
Chapter 4 – We have the right to use One{three} 15
Chapter 5 – Money also is shaped by One{three} 19
Chapter 6 – Leaders need to understand One{three} 25
Chapter 7 – The One{three} helps us live with purpose 31
Chapter 8 – Using the One{three} gives health to our spirit 38
Chapter 9 – The better you use the One{three}
               the more content you are 42

What's The Point? 47
About The Author 53

Other books written by Richard Palmquist

CREATIVE CONFUSION
WHAT ON EARTH ARE YOU IN HEAVEN'S NAME
INTIMACY, GATEWAY TO HELL OR TO GOOD HEALTH
EINSTEIN, MONEY AND CONTENTMENT
(Unpublished) ESCAPE THE CANDY CAGE

---

*"As a man thinks
in his heart, so is he."*
- Proverbs 23:7

His Grandson Needs Help

"Sally sits next to me in school," Gramps. "She's nasty to me. What can I do?"

Eyes lowered, dark mood, my fourteen-year-old grandson touched my hand. He had a problem.

"I have told you how to try to solve problems," I reminded him.

"Tell me again."

"Okay. Everything in life is in a place. In that place is a thing. Tied to, next to, the thing is what can make the thing work. When those three are right, you get something done: you get results."

"I remember. That's what you told me your first book is about."

"That book was three hundred pages of simple stuff that was buried deep in … well, never mind, George. Let's get to work. How do we solve your problem? Tell me about Sally."

"What about her?"

"Do you kind of like her?" Grandpa lifted an eyebrow and smiled.

His face glowed, ears red. "Grandpa! Never mind."

"We have to start somewhere. Tell me, does she make you feel weird?"

"Sort of."

"How do you think you make her feel?" Grandpa smiled. He could be a tease.

"Gramps, how am I supposed to know?"

"Does she smile at you?"

"Frowns." George growled.

"Why?"

"I don't know."

At this point grandpa went into a discussion with George about how he felt about this girl, what she was like. How she and the teacher got along with each other. They learned together that George has reason to believe that Sally gets better grades than George, that she is popular and that she needs to sit at a desk far from George.

"All this we know about Sally is helpful, George. What do you make of it?"

"Aw, Grandpa, please. I don't know. She confuses me."

"Confused? Okay, that's a good place to start. Can you agree that you want Sally to act better toward you?"

"Okay."

"Good! That will be our goal. Maybe Sally will become your friend. Remember what I have told you about solving problems!"

"You mean getting three things to line up?"

"Yes, what are those things? 'Takes three to make one.' Remember?"

"You have to have a 1) thing being 2) moved in a 3) place. Those three form a result."

"Yes. Inside a result is something that just sits there. It has ability but it needs to be moved into action. It can act – fill a need -- only when it is paired with something to push it. The result gets done by an ability being pushed in a place."

"I guess my classroom is the place, but I don't know what the 'thing' is."

"How about the fact that you two are seat mates? You sit next to each other. Is that it?"

"I suppose."

"If the school room is the place and you two are in it, what is moving how you treat each other?"

"Moving how we treat each other? Gramps! I wish I knew."

At this point his mother called him away.

"Wait a second, George. Here's a good example. Your mom can wait."

"Thanks, Gramps. Go ahead."

"In English class what two important parts are in a complete sentence?"

"A noun and a verb."

"What is the noun?"

"It is a person, place or thing. It's something. Oh, I think I know where you are going. The noun sits in the sentence and goes nowhere unless a verb, a mover, gives it action: life. Right?"

"Hey! See, 'Takes three to make one' fits everywhere. Even in English class. Now, scoot. Your mom wants you."

"Got it."

Seems his mother had a chore that was more important than George solving his problem. If the problem George faces were your problem, what would you do? How would you begin to solve it? Here is a clue. Whenever you need to analyze an issue remember the slogan, "Takes three to make one." Figure out the result you want. That's the goal. The three pieces to line up are 1) What is the thing, the issue, the source of ability? 2) What can move that thing? and 3) Where do those two fit? Where can they work together to create your needed result?

This is the kind of job my first book was designed to do. What book? In 2005, I wrote EINSTEIN, MONEY AND CONTENTMENT. I had just come off my life-career. My wife and I had just sold our radio station, purchased an acre near the coast and we were cherishing family and memories of our career in media. We had owned a radio station, a once-weekly newspaper and twice each year we created a telephone directory for each of two communities.

It was time for me to publish deep thinking to help people solve problems: a tool for problem solving. This book is a translation of that complex book. The 2005 book was titled EINSTEIN, MONEY AND CONTENTMENT. Here you will find the points I tried to make back then in simpler language than I used in 2005 and in the second edition in 2013.

A book written to explain a book is not common, unless the first book is a great historic gem. Thousands of books have been written to explain the Bible. Yet, Luther is recognized in history for explaining that the Bible speaks for itself and we do not need a priest to explain it.

Rarely, however, is a book worth much if it requires the author to write another book to explain it. So, this book you are holding is unusual. I take no pride in the fact that my 2005 book has not gone viral. I must confess that fact troubles me. But the useful point of that book is so important I must now swallow my pride and give this subject another try.

Hang on to your hat. This is going to be a trip. In less than a third of the original book's 300 pages I will put cookies on the bottom shelf. You can enjoy this book and profit from it simply by reading it. But if you want to dig deeper, you can match the content of this book with my original by putting both books together. Go chapter by chapter. If you are a digger, you will deepen your understanding of the findings of my work.

Let's get a move on. It would take more effort than I want to spend to repeat "Takes three to make one," whenever I need to remind you of this pattern of thought, so let's make a deal. I don't dare use the shortcut 1=3. Nope. That won't work. So, let's do it this way "One{three}." All through nature there is within every result (desire or plan) -- every "one," or structure, a thing needing a partner to move that thing to create a result. Inside every purpose there is an ability that must be moved. The ability and its mover work together to create a result.

This is a tool. It can be used to get to the root of just about any problem or to solve any issue. But it is only a tool. It takes work to use a tool, but nothing gets done if you don't have the tool or if you use a tool in the wrong way. If you do a quick-read so that you "catch" the problem-solver? All the better.

My 2005 book needs to be filtered. Enjoy the process.

Let's get started.

Chapter One

We all have problems

George is not alone. All of us seek solutions. Our ability to solve problems grows our ability be adults. Only as problem solvers can we succeed in life. A famous person, one who solved a lot of problems, a scholar who became famous beyond fame, bumped his head on this issue.

Albert Einstein faced a problem he was unable to solve.

I wrote about his problem, his failure, in my book. The book you are now reading is about that book and explains the problem you and I can solve. What is that problem? My five intelligent children are college graduates. When I wrote that book years ago, I was confident that they would be able to grasp its message. My daughter, Mary, challenged me. She said, after the book came out, "Dad, please write a children's version of the book, so we can understand it." That is my problem.

What you are reading is my solution, I hope.

My first book explains how it takes three to make one. One{three} helps to solve problems. Yet, the response to it from intellects, if they learned of it, was "who is this writer?" Has his book been peer reviewed? The most deeply scholarly academics earn their salaries not so much based upon their ability to think, to discover or to teach. They earn because they agree with what others have written, what scholars before them believe about discoveries. They are too busy to consider writings that are not previewed by prejudiced professionals. But you aren't prejudiced, so you can "get it."

There are exceptional academics. For example, my son Dr. Stephen Palmquist. You should hear the details of his "out of box" adventure at Oxford University. He thinks outside the box, as did that postal clerk who became the most eminent physicist.

Einstein was, at least at first, outside the box. He was only a simple postal worker. He sold stamps. However, his brilliant thinking, once understood and accepted, became the foundation for less capable academics who at most had made minor suggestions about how the universe works.

Rarely has any book been so important, so worthy, that other books have needed to be written to explain that book. The Bible is the exception. Thousands of books have been published by those seeking to plumb the infinite depts of its wisdom. My book does not need a fraction of that sort of attention.

Instead, it needs what we are planning to do here. What will happen is that we will, one chapter at a time, reflect each chapter of EINSTEIN MONEY AND CONTENTMENT. Dipping into real life, we will draw understanding from the too-deep content of each chapter and we shall find life, display real experience, and feel the verve of how the simple message of the book should be understood.

The true but too-simple One{three} of understanding? Einstein missed it. He looked for a grand pattern that would be true of all aspects of life, of all that can be observed in the Universe. He sought for his grand formula in just one discipline: mathematics.

Now let's get ridiculous. If you want to discover the one simple ingredient present in any food. If you want to understand how a kitchen should work, where will you go to find your answer? Will you study automobiles? Probably not. Yet, Einstein looked for a GRAND system, a formula found everywhere, and he sought that solution in the kitchen of mathematics.

A Grand pattern must look down on all other knowledge. It must be above all: Universal. The scheme to help understand everything is reflected in the way electricity works.

Untamed, electricity courses through stormy weather. It is lightning. The jagged path from cloud to ground is wild Amperage bound by partnered Voltage, lacking boundaries and causing destruction. The creative use of electricity mandates a structure, a path or place, usually a wire, a circuit. A determined Ampere capability can be wrapped in an adequate thrust of Voltage designed to toast bread, or to drive the motor that cools air by moving a ceiling fan, or that causes an electric car to roll down the highway.

This ABILITY joined by a FORCE in a PATH of wire or circuit creates a RESULT and this set of ingredients is not limited to electricity. This pair of conditions crafted within limits of a path working toward a defined purpose is present in every aspect of life.

For George to solve his problem, he should be advised to define the purpose he would like to accomplish in his future relationship with Sally. He needs to define what ability, when moved, can find a place to operate in such a way that his purpose can be made to work.

Will this be easy? Stay tuned. You may discover his solution for yourself.

Chapter Two

A simple tool

Albert Einstein, the postal clerk who became the great physicist, had a problem. The simple view of that problem? He wanted, after he became famous, to discover a scheme, a pattern, that would be common to everything: a Grand Universal Theory, a structure of thought that would fit, placed anywhere.

In German the name "Einstein" means "one container." Ein – "one." Stein – "mug." Was it to fulfill the destiny of his name that Albert Einstein tried to find a single formula that would explain all the workings of the universe? We will never know. However, many men have sought for Einstein's "holy grail:" a formula explaining everything. They call it the "Grand Unification Theory."

Einstein sought that pattern of thought in mathematics, not recognizing that a GRAND theory must be a pattern of thought that embraces everything, not just one field of study. Yes, he had a problem.

Science often is stumped by problems.

Decades ago, when I was in grade school, I would read Flying magazine in the school library. I recall reading the prediction that within twenty years most travel would take place in the sky. Airplanes would replace automobiles and become the chief mode of travel. That didn't work out, did it? Why? Because there are no highways in the sky. There is a lack of patterns in the sky for individual use of air travel: no left lane and right lane; no white lines; no yellow lines; no stop signs or traffic lights.

That problem disabled everybody but TV-myth Jetsons from enjoying a flying car.

Yes, there are ethereal lanes marked out for commercial airlines to use, but the expertise necessary to lay out and to use a place in the sky rules out the average driver. Without place there is no order. Without place there is chaos. So, the prediction that we would sprout wings? It didn't happen. Developers didn't have the skill to put marked lanes in the sky for pilots to steer safely. So, all the "flying cars" would have just been flitting around. The result would have been like bumper cars, only profoundly more serious.

Everything that happens in the heavens, on earth and in microscopic detail involves a "thing" that is "moved." The "thing" gets its usefulness by what I call a thrust, a mover, a dynamic that pushes the ability. Einstein would have found the pattern he sought if he had, in the words of my second chapter, observed natural order. My quest led me to a deep study of the behavior of electricity.

The best example of a thing that is moved is in how electricity works. But electricity moving outside a structure becomes destructive lightning. So, let's take this another step.

Within any system you will find something with ability. Wrapped around the ability is a thrust, a mover. In electricity, Amperage and Voltage work this way. All of what we see, explained simply, is a combination of a substance that is a part of a wiggling wave. All that we experience in light, sound, radio-TV, microwaves, X-rays and other unseen useful benefits are found in the electromagnetic spectrum.

The solid stuff, matter, is also an infinite number of what scientists call "particles" driven by "waves." Those particle and wave work together within a place. In electricity that place can be a wire or other conductor.

The electric or electronic "thing" being "thrust" inside a "place" produces a result we call power or Wattage.

This is the way electricity works. Because the laws governing the behavior of electricity are reliable, and because the structure of electricity is like the structure of everything. we can use our observation of electricity as a model to learn what is true of everything.

Orientals call the thing and mover a yin-yang. Call them what you will, thing and mover work inside a place to accomplish a result. This is the heart of natural law.

Everything in the universe is in its unique place. The place of life is the universe. The universe is the place where Earth lives. It sets our limits. Of course, within the universe there are so many local places that we cannot explore even the edges of our galaxy. The obvious point is that here in our part of the Universe we have our places.

Any thoughtful person, regardless of level of education, should pause here and grasp what this fact means. It means that we are in an impossible position to "know it all." We are inside, not on top of, the Universe. We have a single, relatively small "place" in the grand scheme of things. Thus, we would be arrogant to think that any idea, any tested scientific "proof," is reliable as gravity or of the day-night cycle. Humility should prevent any scientific quest from shouting an absolute "Eureka."

The Apostle Paul put it wisely. We see as though in a mirror: darkly. Back then mirrors were not "high definition." We have been given certainties we are wise to accept in faith; however, we must confess that only the Creator is truly one who is a genuine "know it all."

The scientist who proclaims a certainty, even a proof faithful to the scientific method, should put his finding in the cover of "it seems." However, the One{three} outline gives you a tool for clear thinking, allowing you to focus upon life in a way that will help you solve problems, plan purposes and fulfill your dreams.

Though Louise, George's mother, is unaware of what George has shared with Grandpa she has her own problem. (By the way, I suspect some readers will assume that I am "Gramps." Is that worth a comment from me?)

"How do I get my son to open up?" Louise and Harry are George's parents. Louise is a clerk at the nearby supermarket and Harry is a marketing executive for a Nebraska electronics firm that makes parts for cell phones.

These two provide well for George. They are capable, loving parents. So, why did their son go to grandpa for help? Why not spill out his grief to his parents? Why? Problems are not seen as opportunities. They often are viewed as a lack of merit, a stain on personality, a secret sin or a cloud that refuses to clear us from a feeling of guilt.

We do better to see problems as opportunities. Somehow George saw Grandpa as being a family member who would listen without giving George a hard time.

The content of a problem can take many shapes. George's problem is likely a misunderstanding. Sally does not know George. She may have a hidden desire to know him, or she may see him as someone who lives in the wrong neighborhood. Whatever their problem is, the "thing" about their problem is that they lack an understanding of each other. This fact alone could be whisked away if the two sat face to face and got acquainted. It hasn't happened.

So, what moves the misunderstanding? What causes the condition that exists between these two students to make the problem a difficulty worthy of being called a problem? The driver, the thrust of the misunderstanding is the failure to become acquainted. The structure, the place of this difficulty is obviously their positions, their chair placement, in the classroom. Move one of them to another part of the classroom and the problem might go away.

That done, there might not be a problem. However, something worse could happen. Children can brawl. Kids have a way of acting almost with as much idiocy as do leaders of nations who prefer war, ignoring diplomacy.

Problems solved help develop maturity. They give us the thrill we feel when our eyes open to solutions.

George's mother catches me just after George kissed his mom and took off for school. Harry had gone to his office an hour earlier.

"Dad. I just don't know how you and mom did it?"

"Did what?" Gramps thought he could guess, but he wanted to hear Louise talk about it. Grandpa wanted her to have a chance to spill it out.

"Harry and I are doing okay, but when it comes to George, oh boy. Sometimes I wonder what I have to do to learn how to be a mother who knows what it means to be a mother."

"And you think I know how a mom works?"

"Well you keep telling us about that book you wrote. How it can help solve problems."

"How soon are you going to read it," he smiled.

"Oh, dad! Really. How on earth did you pack so much stuff into three hundred pages? Maybe I could try, but the little I have looked into it? No thanks. It's too deep."

"So, I need to put out a simple, shorter version of it?"

"That would help. Better. Why not just tell me your secret tool? Tell me how problems can be understood in a way that makes them easier to solve."

"Okay. Got three minutes?"

She said he could take a half hour if it would help her work with Harry in a way that could help them be the parents George needs.

"Louise, look."

He put finger-tips on her toaster.

"What does this do?'

"Makes toast."

"How?"

"Well, you put in slices of bread and turn it on and some stuff inside turns red and in a couple minutes you have toast."

"What makes the inside wires turn red?" He asked.

"It's plugged in."

"To what?"

"The wall."

"Wall?"

She just wasn't getting it.

Chapter Three

One{three} fits everything everywhere

It took awhile but Grandpa was able to explain to Louise that the toaster is designed with wire that is too small to have room for its Amps and Volts. Smaller. Not too small. Not small enough to start a fire, but small enough to start a fire if those glowing red wires were out in the open. This subject seems far off from One{three}, but he must have a point.

"That's why the toaster is inside a box, a protected place," he explained.

"Well, thanks," she replied. "I really haven't wondered about that. But now I appreciate what it takes to make toast, I guess."

Before we go on with Gramps' and Louise, let's go back to High School. To get a light bulb to shine, to allow an electric motor to run, to toast bread: to do any electric work, Watts (power) must be there. It is a Watt that does work. What makes the Watt capable? There are two workers: there is Ability (Ampere) and there is Thrust (Voltage).

When the light switch turns on Volt grabs Amp. Volt says, "Wake up sleepy head. I know you can do this, but you need a push from me."

And off they go. However, they cannot just "Go." They need a path, a road: a wire. That wire limits and focuses Amps and Volts. Electricians call the wire's resistance Ohms.

What Gramps is going to explain to Louise is that a toaster works when the wires inside are smaller than wires normally needed by Amps and Volts. The stress is a little bit too much for the wire. That's why the wire gets red. That's why there is heat toasting bread.

Get clear about this. The "pattern" true of everything in life is that everything you can look at, all we can catch of glimpse of, every aspect of the Universe has a place where an ability is being thrust toward a result. Take any problem in your life and define what it is. Find its place, and then ask what could make it work: what ability can be thrust toward the solution you need. Find the place. Define the ability. Look for what can make that ability do its job. But before you do any of that, get a clear view of the result, the solution, that will put you on the right track.

The correct solution to your problem will be a combination of an ability and something that can make that ability do its job, and those two must operate within a place, a structure. Your goal needs {ability, thrust and place}: three parts in harmony with what needs to be done. Find the right combination and you can solve your problem. You can make progress.

Now, on with our story.

"The third chapter of my book explains how One{three}, the problem-solving tool, fits everything everywhere. No exceptions. If you understand the how, you can enjoy toast in the morning. Plus, you can prevent going to the doctor with a burned finger, or worse you can avoid taking apart the toaster, lest you start a fire. It's practical."

"Okay. I will take your challenge. How does it help me when I play the piano?"

"Good question," but before we go down your musical path, let me ask you to think about times when you feel heated up: when a problem becomes a burning issue, like smoldering bread, too black to be called toast."

"I know that feeling."

"Everybody has. When that happens, the reason is that some part of the three is out of balance or not in the right place: the wrong fit. An issue might be too heavy or too hot. If you understand that everything you face has an ideal weight for the ability part of your solution and every ability also has a correct amount of thrust to move the ability: when all that is clear, you have a better chance to get the right result, preventing a breakdown, a fire. You become able to manage the challenges you face."

"You mean when I have a problem walking because I ate too much, my ability to walk can be more healthy if I discipline myself not to eat too much?"

"Brilliant girl! Oh yes. Perfect example. But it applies to everything. It takes sharp thinking to analyze what we face, to discover that a result we want to create might be overweight, out of place, needing to be replaced with a more effective ability, or a more powerful thrust for the ability we choose to use. The point is that we need to find the correct solution to the question 'what ability fits here?' Then, we need to find what matches that ability, that puts life to the ability, thrusting it to become the right result." Grandpa took a deep breath.

"Hey, enough. You asked about pianos. That question may seem tough. But let's get to work." Grandpa was confident.

"I'm game."

"What is the result? After you build a piano, not you; but after the piano factory finishes one, what does it have? What job does it do?"

"Makes music."

"How? Well, inside there are a lot of wires. They are tuned and grouped into octaves."

"But they are silent, aren't they," Gramps teased.

"Yes."

"Silent until what?"

"Until the hammer hits them." Louise was paying attention.

"How does that happen?"

"The musician, the pianist, hits a key."

"Yes. But look over at the piano. How does the pianist pluck those keys? They are just sitting there. And so are the hammers. Looks like we have a complex example of our 'One{three}' involved here, right?" Grandpa was explaining how One{three} is a pattern that fits larger jobs. "The wire in the piano is like Amperage. It has ability. But it doesn't do anything until the hammer hits it," he clarified.

"And the hammer can't hit until the key is pushed down." Loise had the idea.

"Now you get it." Gramps was happy. "Yes, there is one example after another of the structure, thing, thrust, the three working together to make a result. All of them separate, but all working together, to form the structure we call a piano that contains music only when a pianist makes that music happen. The result is either harmony or noise, depending on the circumstances."

"That is so clear, Dad." She was feeling a new understanding how the world works.

"Let's take this to sheet music. Where does it fit in?"

She looked puzzled. "Well it is what gives us the ability to hear music more than once, but it is worthless unless the reader knows how to act when the sheet music is read. Only somebody trained to read it can create music with it."

"So, in the framework of possible music what do we have? We have the sheet music being acted upon by a musical artist. The result can be a solo, a duet, a chamber presentation or a band or orchestra. All kinds of results, separate results, can find sheet music to be helpful. Right."

"So", she paused a moment. "So yes," she smiled.

"Let's figure out how the sheet music was created. Where does that start?" Grandpa was on a roll.

"Ideas. Somebody has to have a melody or a collection of tempos, harmony, maybe lyrics, that fit into the work the composer wants to create. So, how do you match that with the One{three}?"

"Tell me what you think the structure of a composition is." Grandpa probed.

"Well, there is first of all the training and skill of the composer so that he or she knows the rules of music. There can be harmony or discord. There can be beat or a collection of clashing beats, there can be melody, maybe: or there can just be wandering collections of sounds. There has to be content."

"And the composer writes it down. Okay. Now, where does it go from here?"

"Usually, it would go under the seat of the piano bench. It might sit there for a year." Loise is a realist.

"But when a publishing house learns about it and wants orchestras or marching bands to be able to play the composition, what is necessary?"

"First you have to have the original music, the composer's work on paper, or noted in his PC or cell phone. You have to know what the composition is. There has to be something to copy."

"So, if there is a structure of 'This is good and deserves to be usable in public,' you have the music: that's like Amperage and you have the publisher: like Voltage." Grandpa cannot get away from the similarity to how electricity works.

"And the result?" Loise asked.

"The result is a plate that fits into the printing press."

We could keep on like this, one subject after another, and we would never ever finish. This chain of ability moved inside a purpose leading to a result: it is universal. Did you notice how I tried to avoid electrical terms? It is simple and it is everywhere. Everywhere!

The ability is moved with a thrust working toward a purpose. That result could then become an ability in another purpose leading to a third result and that result may become an ability needing to be enabled by something else. It never ends. This is what makes the Universe so complex.

The outline of my book follows the observations we learned from electricity. The thing I keep calling 'ability' is life. It is moved either by spiritual values or by other ideas. We choose. The result, of course, is conditioned by the place we choose, and what results is what the ability-thrust gets done.

In this chapter we have broadened our view of the problem solving One{three} pattern. We will see it not only as a broad observation about the universe, reflected in how electricity works. We apply it to other issues.

The pattern demonstrated by electricity applies to every aspect of knowledge. Nobody is able to explain fully what electricity is. Yet, its laws began to be understood long ago. They are fixed understandings -- not hypotheses – facts not disputed. The laws of electricity and the laws of the universe are expressions of an underlying outline.

The thing and the thrust are so bound up with each other that it is difficult to tell them apart. In the case of electricity, there is no job Amperage (Thing), though available, can do outside the presence of Voltage (Thrust). Voltage can be present in an electrical circuit as a potential, with no Amperage connected. This is the condition when the circuit is not doing work: when there is no load, but then nothing gets done. No result happens. So, we must view the thing and the thrust as closely wedded and joined to do a job.

The ability thing is a nothing, or at least it has no effect, unless it is wrapped in the thrust. The Thing/Thrust pair are nothing in their potential for action unless contained in, limited by, the Place. Together these three create a Result ready to do a job.

Chapter Four

We have the right to use One{three}

When I was beginning my broadcasting career, I heard the Chairman of the Federal Communications Commission, Fred Ford confess that he had a problem with government regulations. He told us about a poem during a speech at a convention in Washington, D.C. Even though Ford was Chairman of a government agency that regulated broadcasting, he saw regulations as humorous and sometimes non-sensical.

He was telling us about his frustrations with the way regulations in government tend to discourage creativity. When the composer finds the flow of art, when the entrepreneur meets the first investors, when the well-intentioned young politician builds a support group, all too often government's response is warm and its prohibitions are severe.

Here is the poem he learned from his mother.

> Mother dear may I go down to swim?
> Yes, my darling daughter.
> Hang your clothes on the hickory limb
> But don't go near the water.

George and Grandpa had a talk about Chairman Ford's poem.

"So, you have ambition. In spite of the opposition and other frustrations a business owner experiences you still want to be sure to get an education that to help you start your business. Let's see how that fits into our One{three} of problem solving, how it helps you cope with troubling regulations. Get me started."

"I don't know how to start. Sure, there will be problems, but I just want to make a lot of money."

"I thought so. Where would that money come from? Your investors?"

"At first, I suppose."

"How will you pay dividends or if they lend you money, how will you pay off those loans?"

"Frankly, I haven't thought about that. I'm glad you are bringing it up. I suppose, in general, the way I would do that would be to make sales."

"Sales of?"

"Of whatever my business deals in."

"Deals in what, George? What will you sell?"

"Whatever we end up making."

"So, yours will be a manufacturing company? Right?"

"Well, maybe."

"If not, then what? What would you be doing if you didn't manufacture what you sell?"

"We would sell some stuff others make. Like, what if I wanted to sell cars?"

"That's good if you sell cars people in your town want to buy. Better choose the right brand."

"Give me some hints, Grandpa. How do I make a decision like that?"

"I should ask you that question."

"You would! Well, I guess first I would make sure I had a group of people on my team, people with money to invest. Probably, I would have to be satisfied only to own a part of the business."

"That's realistic. Yes."

"Then I would shop around town and find an acre or so of land where hundreds of cars drive by every day. That would be my structure, my place."

"Good thinking. Then what?"

"Well, I would have to figure out what kind of car is not for sale in town, or maybe I would decide to set up a used-car lot at first, where I could help people get a better deal than a new-car place offers."

"How does that fit our One{three} of problem solving? The place is your lot. What is the "ability" part?"

"I think I answered that. The brand of new car would be one choice, or the decision to specialize only in used cars. That would be what I would be able to do: my thing, my ability."

"Right. Yes. Now, what makes your thing go?"

"Go?"

"Yes. What will motivate people to come to your car lot instead of somebody else's place?"

"I don't understand. There would be cars on the lot, looking good, washed clean every morning, tuned up and ready to roll. I would have a big sign out front that would make me look like I know what I'm doing. What am I missing?"

"You won't have any shoppers unless you push your ability to meet a need: unless you move that product cleverly. You will need thrust."

"Clever? What are you talking about?"

"If you go on radio and TV and in the newspaper just telling people, 'Got to get a new car? Buy it from me,' they will pass you by and go shop somewhere else."

"When I graduate, Gramps, how much money will you invest in my car lot idea? I need you on my team."

"Talk to me about that when you have a business plan. And in that plan, you had better have a place containing a unique ability that will work, matched with thrust, and it better bring a profitable result. That result will not happen unless you have the skill to learn what your prospective customer is thinking, what that customer-group believes it needs. Unless you have empathy. Got it?"

"You are tough, Grandpa, but yes, I get it."

Einstein is quoted as saying, "Concern for man himself and his fate must form the chief interest for all technical endeavors. Never forget this in the midst of your diagrams and equations." He had a practical understanding of life along with his deep thoughts. Einstein has been viewed as floating above mankind in a cloud of foggy mathematical formulas disconnected from everyday life. But he seemed to have common sense.

So, what was Einstein's reason for his quest for a Grand Unification Theory? Would it be fair to guess that he hoped to be able to help better the living conditions of mankind? Did he want to cast light on a new view of Economics? Whether Einstein wanted to apply his thinking to Economics is beside the point. We can see in his search the desire to provide a path for such an inquiry. My pattern of all is that path.

As my pattern of all, found in the laws of electricity applies to everything, those fixed laws of electricity become applicable to the practical field of Economics.

Chapter Five

Money also is shaped by One{three}

Normal grandsons would never think of inviting grandpa to speak to his class at school. Dread the thought. George is not quite normal. You might say he is above normal.

After his deep talks with his grandfather, George actually got permission from Miss Andre, his teacher, to invite George's grandfather to talk to his government class. It's called civics. Interesting title for instruction about a function that so often behaves without civility. But then …

The day came. George told Miss Andre that she should introduce Grandpa. She had insisted that George be the one to tell his classmates about his grand-dad, but George seemed so embarrassed at the idea that the teacher caved in.

"Today, we are going to be hearing some information from a man with a lifetime of experience in business. He is the father of George's father."

Miss Andre gave Grandpa a nod.

After light applause, half the kids looking out the window, Grandpa stood in front and looked over the class. He took his time. First, he looked stern, sour faced. Then gradually, he curled his expression into a warm, friendly smile.

"Did you bring your lunch today?"

Grandpa knew the school in this small town had no cafeteria. There was just a small lunch room with vending machines.

"Raise your hand if you did." The hands of several went up and he went on: "Where did that lunch come from?"

There was a silent pause.

"Mom," came from the back row. The class thought that was hilarious. It took a moment for the laughter to die down.

"Okay. I guess I stumped you. You can say Mom created your lunch. Obvious and true, but that's not the point. Where did that food come from?"

"Farms," somebody offered.

"Oh, your dad goes out to a farm and picks raspberries and digs potatoes?"

Laughter.

"Your food comes from money! I heard a funny story once about a family that moved from a big city to a rural town like this and they bought a house with an orange tree in the front yard. A neighbor came to greet the new family. He approached the newcomer and said, 'The folks who moved out of your house would let our kids eat oranges from your tree. Would that be okay with you?'"

"Oranges? Are these oranges? Oranges from a tree? No!" The new neighbor went on: "From a tree? I don't think so. Wouldn't that be dangerous? Oranges we eat come from stores."

Now the class was really involved. The laughter burst into shouts, and it took a while before they calmed down.

Grandpa continued, "The poor fellow went on, 'The oranges you eat? They have to come from grocery stores.'"

"I don't know how those neighbors solved that problem, but some people have strange beliefs about how we get stuff." Grandpa smiled.

"One thing is certain, though. We have to have money to have food. We need money to buy food, unless we are farmers. And farmers can't produce food without the money to buy farm equipment. Money is what allows us to have a place to live, to have food to eat, clothing to wear and to go on vacations. Money is what gives us ability. Where does that money come from?"

Grandpa then went into a brief summary of how he wrote about money in his book. He explained how we get manufactured stuff, plus paying doctors and dentists, nurses and other people for helping us: all that makes up a prosperous society. The goods and services not only cost money, but there is a mystery behind where money comes from.

"Money is created from a policy of government and it comes to us by a Federal government process. The money policy of government is what gives money its value and the process makes it possible for manufacturers and businesses to do business and for retailers to set prices," Grandpa explained.

"A long time ago people used to live simple lives. Their houses didn't amount to much and most of them lived out on farms. Some would raise cattle, others hogs; some would grow corn, others cotton. When a dairy farm owner needed a new shirt, he might go to the cotton grower and he would offer some milk in return for a fair amount of spun cotton. He might even have to barter for a bushel or two of just plain cotton bolls. If that happened, he would have to go to a place in town where somebody had a special machine that would spin the cotton into fabric. Then, somehow, he would have to get that fabric into the hands of a seamstress who knew what he wanted in the way of a new shirt. There was nothing simple about that, because in those days the only thing people had to spend was what they grew or what they made.

"It didn't take all that long for leaders in the town to get the idea that everybody needed to trade with only one product, a valuable item, easy to carry around. At first, they didn't even use the word money. Did they ever come up with some weird ways of agreeing on what they would use for trading! After a while it became clear that there were some metals, like silver and gold, that had value: you could make something out of them, but they don't decay, they didn't get sour like a bucket of milk. They held their value.

"If any of you kids decide to go into banking you will take college classes about how all that worked. You can learn the details, but what we live in today is a step beyond just having money.

"It used to be that a government could only print a dollar bill if they had a certain amount of silver or gold: if they really did have it in storage. That system of money gives paper money the same value as the metal money. The adventures over that system? Those stories fill lots of books.

"Beginning in the early 1900's a group of bankers got together and worked out a plan for governments to be able to print money on paper even though they didn't have gold and silver. No silver. No gold. But they still printed money and they got people to accept that money as though it could be traded for gold or silver. They fooled whole nations into having that idea."

A voice in the back shouted, "You mean they cheated?" The class roared in laughter.

"A lot of sincere people have that opinion, but cheating or not, the process is blessed by the governments of the world and at least for now it seems to work." Grandpa gave a broad smile, a teasing grin.

"One lesson, one thing you will learn for sure, if you study economics in college: the more money out there ready to be spent, the more stuff is going to cost. Lots of money in a country means bread will cost more than it did when less money was circulating. It is a simple rule that can't be broken.

"When I was a child in the Midwest, my dad could buy a loaf of bread for three pennies. Today, that same bread costs more than a hundred times that much. Somebody tell me why."

There was a long pause. The students glanced here and there in stunned silence.

"Who is going to help with this?" Grandpa challenged.

A young lady in the first row was timid, but she spoke up. "I guess today the government must have more money out there than it did when your dad and mom were raising you."

"Yes, by the trillions. True. However, when more people are born, that means more shoppers, more car owners and more people needing a place to live must have money. The more births, the more families developing, the more people shopping, the more money must circulate in order for wages to allow people to meet their needs. So, the amount in circulation has to increase. But rising prices prove that the governments of the world are creating a lot more money than it takes to keep up with population growth.

"What most government employees who are employed by the Treasury Department or the Federal Reserve or the Controller of the Currency or the others in government who control the supply of money may not really 'get' is that money has value controlled by a law of nature.

"The money supply is what I am talking about. George will know what I mean when I talk about how money is created. Money has the ability to help people. That ability just sits there, unused, until it is thrust into circulation. It has to be earned or borrowed, spent, in order to produce increased prosperity. That purpose then becomes a new part of another pattern.

"The function that gives value to money has two parts. It is first of all, how much stuff is for sale? Then, how much money is in the hands of customers? Those two together provide guidance to the people who create money, Congress and the agencies involved. They look at the balance between what is for sale and how much money is out there and this gives them the ability to decide how much money to create. It is complex, but that's the pattern. You can learn more if you get my book EINSTEIN, MONEY and CONTENTMENT.

"George wanted me to meet you because he has learned about that book I wrote back in 2005. It goes deeply into this whole subject and I mean really deep."

Grandpa closed by telling the class how they can encourage their parents to buy his book. He shook hands with Miss Andre, and off he went, satisfied that he left those students full of questions about money and what it is worth.

"Absolutely…" he proclaimed, waiving an arm and spreading a smile to each student. "… it was fun being with you today." *

---

* To learn more about how money is created, ask for my unpublished booklet "Escape the Candy Cage." Write to richardpalmquist@gmail.com. If you are reading this at a time when my email address has become "un-Googled," by then you may be able to find "Candy Cage" as a published book.

Chapter Six

Leaders need to understand One{three}

"Gramps, I need to have a long talk with you. A lot of my friends are talking about what they want to do in life. How they are going to earn money." It was George. He was giving more thought to his future career.

"Been there. Heard them, George. So, what are your latest thoughts about your future?"

"I will tell you first what I have decided I don't want to do. These guys, even a few of the girls in my class? They talk about how much an hour they will earn, or what kind of a big salary they will get if they work for the government."

Grandpa chuckled. "Hey, that's a really puzzling point you bring up. Why does working for the government come out in the same sentence with large salary."

"That's the way things work."

"I know. But why?"

"Why? Well, you tell me. Isn't government more important than maybe a career as a doctor?"

"Politicians would agree with that idea. But think about it. What does government produce? I will answer the question. The government's job is always negative. Government tells us what we must not do unless we want to be punished. That's the job government does inside the country. And it is an important job."

George's eyes lit up. "Just like the way the people across the street get visited so often by the cops, right?"

"Exactly. But outside the country. What does government produce? Well. This is more complicated. Government creates warships, aircraft carriers, assault rifles, training camps, all kinds of military stuff. That's the main thing government manufactures, and we have to be able to defend ourselves, but how does that kind of manufacturing plant put food on the table or computers on our desks?"

"Is that really all they do?"

"There is one other job, George. Government also sits on top of a pile of money. An infinite amount of it. The job of managing our money to compete with the money made by other countries: that's a huge job. But though we have to have a trustworthy dollar to spend, that job is about caution. It's not about creating new stuff. But you have something in mind. What's your question? How are you thinking a different way than the guys at school?"

"Grandpa, I don't want to get paid by the hour. I don't want to work for government either, unless I have to get drafted into the army. So, what is involved in my getting ready to run my own business?"

"Without knowing it you have brought up the subject I deal with in Chapter 6 of my book. Right on target. In that chapter I show how important it is to have a good education, training that will allow you to get into the kind of work that fits best. I show that to find that special place in life you need ambition."

"I might have too much of that."

"Well, the old Katzenjammer Kids comic when I was a kid used to repeat, 'Too much is enough,' or something like that. Good for you."

"Anyhow, Education, ambition and empathy. Those are the keys to getting into business, to being a leader."

"That helps. But it's all kind of general. What's the structure – you would say the 'place' of -- leadership? Yes, I remember your One{three} of problem solving. Inside a place there is a thing that is able and it needs a thrust. The result is the solution to the problem. Just like in electricity. Got it."

"Good for you."

"So? How about it? My problem is I want to be a leader. What is my solution?"

"Do you know what a Sputnik is? Ever heard of it?"

"Not from science class. We learned about it in Civics. The Russians beat the United States to space with Sputnik?"

"Right. Draw me a picture of it."

George looked startled.

"Don't look at me that way. Do it."

"Not that hard. Okay," George agreed.

While George doodled, Grandpa went on, "Back in Junior High School we were taught that the highest mankind had risen above the earth's surface was 5,000 feet. A lot has happened since then."

"I'll say! Here's the Sputnik." George had produced a circle with four lines extending from the outside of the circle, evenly spaced."

"That's what it looked like," Grandpa nodded. "It was launched when Kennedy was President. I remember the challenge he gave us in his radio news conference announcing the Sputnik launch. He decided to see the cup both half-empty and half-full. He detailed the way the United States was behind. He called it a 'leadership gap.' Yet, he projected hope:

Have Only Positive Expectations, my words, but a good verbal description of Kennedy's attitude.

"That was in 1957. I was in the midst of starting a major business back then and I knew I had to pay attention to how to be a leader. Kennedy went on to proclaim that we needed to have schools filling up with young people who could learn the science involved in conquering space."

George interrupted. "I don't get it. What does the Sputnik have to do with leadership?"

"Great question. My point is that I was stunned by Kennedy's challenge. Stunned that I did not know what it meant to be a leader. What parts does a house have? I could answer that. What are the parts of a car? I could get some of them. But the parts of leadership? Nope. I had no idea."

"But you came up with some help, I bet. How?"

"This may sound unreal, but after Kennedy's speech I prayed. I asked the Lord to tell me what I needed to know about leadership."

"And ..."

"I am going to give it to you one word at a time."

"Okay."

"Here we go. Take your pen and write on the upper left line of the Sputnik. You know that those four lines are radio antennas, right?"

"I don't know why they had to have four, but yes. Two on each side each one opposing one on the other side of the big ball that had the equipment in it. So, what do I write?"

"Upper left, write LISTEN."

"Got it."

"Over on the lower right side write SPEAK. So, a leader listens and he or she speaks. Then on the lower left write READ and on the upper right put the word WRITE."

"What word fits in the center of the circle?"

"The most important word. Write THINK. A leader knows first how to listen. Did you take a course in grade school about how to listen?"

"No."

"Major corporations call in experts, some of them do, and they hold seminars teaching employees what it takes to be a good listener. The point is that a leader is a listener."

"Hey, I think I get it. If you listen that means you have information to speak about, or at least if you don't listen you really have nothing important to say. Right?"

"Absolutely. So, a leader listens and speaks and he also reads and writes."

"And in the middle of all that information coming in and going out? I get it! A leader has something to think about. Informed thinking."

"That's what makes a leader. Yes."

"But Gramps, how does this fit your One{three} for problem solving?"

"It shows that even though finding an ability that can be active within a structure to create a result, in spite of how simple it seems, the way it works is really complex. Everything that this pattern creates becomes a part of some other similar pattern. That means all we see in telescopes and what is on the glass of a microscope, all that is a complex interworking of just the simple outline: there is a place where there is an ability and that ability has a partner that moves it in a structured place, creating a result."

"Okay, but you haven't answered me. How do Sputnik's five words fit in that outline?"

"Think about it this way. There are two outlines. The Sputnik has an ability called listen being driven by a speaking. These two fit in a place called the public. The leader becomes a leader when he or she becomes a respected public speaker. The result (in electricity, the power) is the degree of public respect the leader stirs up.

"That's really good. Whew. But what about 'read and write'?"

"Those two are similar but they are part of the leader's private life, the inner preparation for leadership. Public impact needs private reading and writing. In order to be able to listen and speak you need the nourishment you get from reading. Once you are a capable reader, you can express yourself in writing. All this is within the pattern, the place, of clear thinking."

"Tell me how to put my leadership ability into a new project. Not that I have one in mind. Just give me a general hint."

"Thanks. I am glad you asked. This is another thought that came to me when I was just starting business, after school. Thinking deeply about how to get money to start a business, I got this outline, shaped in a horseshoe pattern. Motivation, Money, Men. Good ideas don't always have to begin with the same letter, but it helps."

"Okay, but I don't get what you are driving at."

"I'm not surprised. Let me explain. Motivation is my key word for the 'idea that would meet a human need: something that would sell.' That comes first. Next you have to get a little money together to make the thing or to make the concept known. Whatever expenses it will take to get the business to start moving: that money is next. Finally, in this first round, you hire men, the do-it-people, men and women, who will start up the business, using that money."

"Just to show you I get it. I would guess what you are going to say next is that after the business starts, you re-do the motivation part, expand the plan and make the thing bigger, meaning you need more investment money and more workers. Right?"

"Sharp kid, you are. But I knew that."

"Grandpa, do you think I need to read Chapter Six of your book to make it work?"

"Probably not."

Chapter Seven

The One{three} helps us live with purpose

Gramps stayed overnight. The alarm in the bedroom upstairs startled him. At home this old fellow needs no alarm. It was too early for him to think about coffee, but he was a guest this morning, so he kicked off his covers and shuffled to the window.

The autumn leaves hung in colorful indecision. Should they stay attached to the trees or was it time for them to follow the fashion of the season and flutter to the ground to decay into food for next spring's fresh start?

A fresh start for this day felt good to the old man and before he thought more about it, coffee warmed his lips as he heard Harry stomp down the stairs.

"I'm not like you," Gramps boasted, "Nobody cares if I wear shoes. Nobody cares if my shirt is still in the closet. How did you sleep?"

"Okay."

"As usual, I suspect. Where's Louise? Is she up yet?"

"She's catching a few more winks. It will be an hour before George has to be ready for school."

"Is it fun for you? Your job? Are you happy there?"

Harry was pouring a bowl of Rice Crispies. He looked sadly at the floor, as if checking his shoelaces.

"Why do you ask?"

Gramps had visited his son's family over the weekend and slept on the couch Sunday night. He saw a Monday morning dread clouding his son's face. "You seem a little down."

"Maybe I am more than a little down. I have a huge problem at work. I don't know how to sort it out."

"Nobody doubts your electronic engineering skill, Harry, I am sure of that. So, it must be … Well, you tell me."

"The company gets good value for my effort. Sure. No problem. But the stress and distraction make me work ten times harder and check my work twice as much as I would need to. The problem is that my boss really does stupid things."

"Ever heard of the Peter Principle?" Gramps knew a lot about how organizations work.

"Wasn't that Laurence Peter? Back in 1969, he and his partner studied how corporations worked. I remember! Yes. You hit the nail on the head. My boss is a perfect example. Yup. He did so well as director of merchandising that they advanced him to manager of engineering. He is way out of his skill level. Knows nothing about what we have to do, but he just is absolutely positive that he knows more than he needs to know. The Peter principle says that in big organizations if you keep doing a good job you will end up getting promoted to a job that is above your ability to perform."

"Sounds like he's a pill. Does he act like a tyrant?"

"Not exactly. He just sets goals and demands that he should realize are beyond reason." Harry had not started to eat his cereal.

"Let's eat. What are you having?" Harry asked, turning toward Grandpa.

"I saw Wheaties in the cabinet. Is that okay?"

"Sure. Just be relaxed. You're always welcome here."

"Harry, you do remember all I have told you about what the Bible says about liberty. Right?"

"You have a chapter about that in your book. More detail than I need, but what does that have to do with my problem?"

"Maybe nothing. But it could have a lot to do with your future. What is your goal? You going to try to get that boss fired? If you did get him fired, would that solve your problem?"

"I don't plan to shoot him. That's for sure. And the President of the company? He plays golf every Saturday with my boss. What chance would I have to go over his head? I'd get my head chopped off."

"You're right."

The two men were interrupted by Louise. "Happy Monday morning, Gramps," she grinned.

"You too. George up yet?"

"Barely, but he will be down soon. What are you too so deep into?"

Harry scowled, wondering inside whether he dared tell his father how the work problem was impacting his relationship with Louise. "Oh, you know, honey. The boss. What else."

Gramps saw a chance to plant some ideas that would help these two use his problem-solving One{three}. "Okay kids," he said, "Enjoy breakfast. I finished my cereal. Let's have some fun with this big problem at work. I can see it's hurting both of you."

Louise ripped, "You don't know the half of it. This husband of mine can't keep work at work. He loads it off on me every night when he comes home. It is really getting old."

"Let's back off a little." Grandpa suggests. "In order to focus on a problem, we need to get an idea of where the problem fits in our lives. Tell me. You believe in the Lord. You both know God is all-powerful. Right?"

"So?" Harry snapped.

Louise added, "Sure. Where are you going with this?"

"The Ruler of the Universe has this super-human ability. He is lot like a GPS. Ever think of that? You get in the car knowing where you want to go, but not knowing how. Across the street, a neighbor is starting a fifty-mile trip using the same GPS. That GPS seems to be everywhere and it has no problem serving hundreds of differing requests at the same time. That algorithm is as close to infinity as any human has ever reached: God, though, is really everywhere and everywhere able. All powerful. Everywhere powerful.

"The GPS we use in our cars is controlled by an algorithm, a pre-set imperfect observation about where you are located and an equally imperfect plan to get you where you want to go. Many have been told by a GPS to go around the block when a U-turn would have done the job.

"God's indwelling Holy Spirit is living intelligence with a perfect understanding of where you are, a clear view of where you have been and perfect advice you are free to follow: advice that will get you where you should go."

Grandpa asks, "When you two received the Lord as your Savior, what did that mean about you and the Holy Spirit?"

Loise was the first to reply. "The Holy Spirit is inside us."

"Okay. The GPS is in your car and ready to serve you when you need help getting somewhere you haven't gone before. Right? In the same way, only more-so, the Holy Spirit is in your cells, in your heart, in your mind, in your personality – in you. Let's go back. How powerful is the Holy Spirit? Any limit to His ability?"

Harry replies. "Totally powerful. All the way."

"So," Gramps went on: "Where is that ..."

Louise interrupted, "I get it! The Holy Spirit lives in us. So how come we are so powerless? Why do we have to struggle? If we have the Ruler of the Universe in us, and both of us do, why do we battle over issues? How come the Holy Spirit seems to tell Harry one thing and me something else? When he comes home grouched about work, why doesn't he have the power ..."

"Hey, wait," Harry defends himself. "Just a minute. You are giving dad the idea that when I come home after a stress-day at work, you are the pretty smiling babe ready to make me feel all warm inside. You've got your problems too."

Gramp spoke, leaning back a little in his kitchen chair, "If the Ruler of the Universe ..." He restarted, "Wait. Let's look at it this way. If the GPS is in your glove compartment, is it going to tell you how to get to the beach? Probably not. Maybe there are places you already know how to get to. True. Maybe you don't always need the GPS. Does it pounce on you? Does it turn on when the engine starts and yell at you, 'What's up for today?' How about it? Answer me."

They were silent.

"If we have the power to bathe and we neglect it. Guess what. We radiate BO. If we complain that our toenails keep cutting holes in our socks and we just keep on ignoring the job of clipping them, what do we expect? We have to buy new socks. We have a part in this business of life. You can ignore the GPS and it won't complain. You can use it and decide you know a better path and you are going to waste a lot of time correcting your path. Get it?"

Harry scowled. "You know. I never thought of that. Good grief. The Creator of the Universe is a power millions of times the strength of any silly GPS. His infinite ability is inside of each of us when we invite Him to live in us."

Louise adds, "He sure is. Wow. We can really be stupid sometimes, can't we?"

Grandpa smiles, "You are getting the picture. Just like the GPS is a willing servant, not a master, the Holy Spirit inside each of us is a welcome courteous ability inside."

"Why doesn't He take control?"

Harry complained. "Why does he let us do such stupid things, to have such miserable stress, fail to think clearly – have fights? How come He allows all that?"

"We don't need to ask Him," Gramps smiled. "He has already told us. That's what we learn by reading how He dealt with Adam and Eve, with Noah, with Abraham, with all the big guys we learn about in the Bible's history books. He refuses to treat us like robots. We are free. We have been given individual liberty. Look! For whatever reason, God has the need to be respected. Someday, that need might become more clear to us, but the point is that God cannot do what He wants to do with us if it is only Him doing it.

"He needs us to get a clear vision of His will and His pattern, His world-view, his principles, laws: the way He wants things done. Once we rub against life enough to learn how not to do things, He wants us by our own experience to learn how to fit into His will, His pattern for our lives. When we have the right attitude? That's when He can chime in. That's when His eternally powered Divine GPS for our lives can give us direction. The direction is there. It is usable. But God normally keeps His hands off the steering wheel."

Harry smiles, "Where are you going with this, Dad? Are you suggesting that these new self-driven cars are tools of the Devil?"

The three have a good laugh.

Let's break in here and observe that Grandpa has yet to deal with solving Harry's work problem, but he has raised a basic working thought to help the family get to the next step.

Let's look at the "One{three}" as it applies to this conversation so far. Grandpa has examined the structure of the spiritual life of his son's family. He has observed that his son, the wife and their child are all living with the Holy Spirit in their lives. The structure of the family has two elements in it. His son, wife and the child, each one of them, has the eminent ability of the Universe living inside. That power is like Amperage in an electrical circuit. The structure of each family member is like Ohms in the way electricity works. The Voltage within each of them has been declared by the Creator to be personal individual liberty: willpower.

Our decisions, our will, give us the choice of living life depending upon the Holy Spirit. Or the Holy Spirit can be latent within us, doing nothing. That is a choice each of us is allowed to make. The ease of solving our problems, the power available to rise above life's difficulty, depends upon how we use our will power to access God's eternal capability, His direction-finding. He is willing to enrich our lives and to allow us to get results, to fulfill purpose. Or if we choose, He can simply be available, like Amperage waiting be connected to a load, inside but not active. God does not use us as puppets. Neither is He our puppet. However, He is the Creator of the Universe. To ignore His direction? That seems to be absurd. The decisions we make determine the result: Wattage (power) bringing success, or lacking correct decisions, the dread of life's failures.

The point Grandpa was making is something we all need to take seriously. If we want to solve life's problems, it helps to know that we have the most powerful, the wisest, the most caring, most loving power in the Universe within us, a part of us, not just a part but in a sense the source of all we need to know, the wisdom we need. He is not just the spiritual Google available to us, all knowing, but He is the One who knows what will happen if we go the wrong way on the highway of life. He is available to us to help us find "green pastures" of joy, to experience the dancing waters of genuine fun, to find the fulfillment of purposes and to look back with satisfaction that the rock-filled snowballs of life have each melted, leaving nourishment we call wisdom.

George appeared. "I got up a little early," he smiled. "Heard you guys down here talking some really heavy stuff. But Gramps. We do have problems. The Lord knows we have these troubles that need solutions. How come He allows our lives to get so messy sometimes?"

"Good question," George. "How would you answer your son, Harry?"

"Well, uh maybe: I guess the answer to that question is that the problems we solve today become the tools we use to solve more important problems tomorrow. Is that about it, Dad?"

"Good answer. So, let's get to work on the problem created by your boss. Do you think the Holy Spirit is smart enough to help you find a solution? What is your solution? That comes first. Can you find a pleasant relationship with your boss? If not, are you confident that you can find another job? Whatever you decide, keep in mind that the structure for your solution is the welfare of your family life.

"Within that framework you need to develop in yourself enough empathy to realize that whomever is your boss that person has a personality, a unique set of qualities that make him or her who they are. That is the relationship you want to be certain is harmonious.

"Get to that point, and you will come home happy at night."

My One{three}, my concept of the principle that underlies everything in life, helps to define contentment, a step beyond happiness. Originally, I had intended to make the thesis of my original book a study of prosperity.

Contentment is more important.

Chapter Eight

Using the One{three} gives health to our spirit

Across the street from the pleasant house where George and his family live is a house that looks like their house but it is different. The house of the Wanamaker family is noisy. There are two adult women living there and George tried to count once. He thinks there are seven children. It appears there are four teenaged sons and three daughters. Sons? Daughters? Well maybe.

They are not adults and they behave in the neighborhood as though it will be a long time before they can earn a living and build their own families.

The two adult women work during the day and a man who is a mystery to neighbors cares for the house when he is capable. He putters around the front yard from time to time and it appears he must be father to at least a few of the children. Nobody knows for sure, and we don't need to go there.

This domestic settlement, is that what it is called, is well known to the local police department. The black and white patrol cars need no

GPS to find the house and late at night the sirens grow louder and really who knows whether the "father" is mistreating one of the women? Who knows whether it is the children who are misbehaving?

The point is that in his neighborhood there is disfunction.

There is an important word in this part of my 2005 book. The word, "contentment." These neighbors are not content. That much is clear. In this chapter we are dropping in on Harry as he discusses the neighbors with his wife and son George.

"The cops are out there again, Harry," his wife begins. "What can we do? Is there something we are supposed to do?"

"It bothers me," Harry confessed. "What should we do when people near us need help, when they are messing up our lives?"

George was not so concerned about what his parents were obligated to do. "Well, there are three parents over there, two kids each, I guess. Isn't it their job to work out their own problems?"

At this point we must stop and sort out what is going on. There is a problem across the street. Nothing unclear about that. Is there also a problem with George's father? Should he be doing something about his feeling of obligation?

It seems we have two problems. First, we need to solve the problem being experienced by George's family. We will have to confess that we don't have enough information to analyze and solve the turmoil across the street.

What then IS the problem being experienced by the three peace-needing people in George's family? George's father has only a vague concept that the problem across the street is personal to his family. However, it is possible that a few days from now he could have a different opinion. That hassle over there in one of the battles could burst into violence. Who knows if that man of the house, vodka bottle in hand, might come out in his front lawn one day pursuing policemen and spray bullets, wounding George?

Are these peace-loving people supposed to prevent future possibilities? In Genesis, God asked Cain, one of the two sons of Adam and Eve, about his murdered brother. In response, Cain, speaking of Abel, asked God,

"Am I my brother's keeper?" The response was inappropriate in the setting of Cain's guilt. However, the remark accurately reflected the fact that we in truth do not have responsibility for our neighbors. Each of us is responsible only for ourselves.

It is time for us to be reminded of a subject in the EMC book. What did chapter eight deal with? Under the heading of Contentment, this chapter was about Love Faith and Grace. The point of it is that if you want to be content, you should recognize that within the framework of faith, love is thrust to action by an attitude of grace.

Now let's see what's happening. The doorbell just rang.

"Grandpa, is that you," George exclaimed.

"I was driving home from grocery shopping and thought maybe you guys needed some support. I heard the sirens. What's going on."

"We don't know," George answered.

"Same old stuff, Dad," Loise offered.

"Grandpa, we wonder whether there is something we can do to get this neighborhood back the way it used to be, before that pack moved in. They are something!" It was George who explained.

Harry moved from the chair of honor and Grandpa sat down.

"Hey, this is a perfect chance to see if my problem solving four-point One{three} can work," Grandpa observed. Where do we start? Let's see."

"What do we want to happen?" George chimed in. "That's where we start. What should the result be?"

"You tell me." Gramps retorted.

"A peaceful neighborhood," Louise suggested.

"Right!" They all spoke at once.

"What is the framework, the structured 'place' of a peaceful neighborhood, George?" Grandpa tested.

"Well, Gramps, they are out there across the street right now. Law and order. Cops give society the structure that encourages people to behave themselves." George hit the nail on the head.

"Absolutely right, son," Grandpa was proud.

"Now, Harry, tell me what it takes within law and order for people to be respectful and peaceful with each other. Tell me."

Harry put his head in his hands and took a while to respond. "I suppose for a family it would be love: respect and love. Respect would be like the Amps in electricity: the ability. Love would be the Voltage, thrust."

"Good answer, son. Now back off. Forget families. How about the group of families? What is necessary for groups of families to have if they live under an orderly set of laws? What do they need for them to live in peace with each other?"

The room fell silent. They all were in deep thought.

Grandpa cleared his throat. "In my book, I suggest that love is joined by faith and grace. Maybe you should ask yourselves how your faith is able to reach across the street and apply grace to that troubled bunch of hoodlums. Would that work?"

Louise responded: "Looks like you have in mind giving me a job: putting the solution to this problem in my lap."

"Why do you say that?"

"Well. The way I get it, what you are suggesting as the answer to this problem is that if we want peace in this neighborhood, we are going to have to find the faith, the expectation of success, to show a smile to those people. Show them grace. Tell them we like them anyhow. Give them the idea that whatever they do, they can count on us to be their friendly neighbors."

"Okay," Grandpa saluted. "You guys need to have your supper and I need to get home. Louise, you are absolutely right. You guys can solve that problem if you take that action."

Harry rose from the couch. "Let me see you to the door, Dad. You know you have put a big burden on Louise, but I agree with you, and I will tell you what. If those people across the street reject our offer to have them over for a friendly meal, well then, I will prod you to get over there and tell them that the problem belongs to them. How about that?"

They both chuckled.

Chapter Nine

The better you use the One{three} the more content you are

After listening to this family's struggles, we leave them, knowing they now better understand how to solve their problems.

But Harry has another one. He began: "Dad, both of us admire the way you have handled the years since you retired."

"It didn't just happen," his father replied.

"I was there, dad. I know. I remember."

"It took some doing alright," Grandpa noted, "but you could not possibly remember all that went into it. The planning, the decisions, tough ones, and all the mistakes your mom and I made."

"Give me an example."

Grandpa mused for a moment, sorting memories. He tossed his head back against the pillow of the La-Z-Boy chair. "Frankly, I'd rather be sorting out your questions than looking back on what I did. But one advantage I have is that the mistakes I made planning to retire, those memories – oh boy – those pains, I can tell you exactly how to suffer if you want."

The couple chuckled.

"Okay, dad, I'll give you a thought starter. We have been stashing some extra cash for a few years now, investing in some stocks. I think we have maybe $150,000 invested, plus the equity in our house. Is that a good start?"

"Well, son," Grandpa's scowl deepened, and he leaned forward. "If you want to live in a one room apartment after you retire and live on beans and grapefruit, it might do."

"We need more."

"A lot more these days. You know that the more money the government spends the more extra you have to pay for potatoes and corn. Right?"

"Yep. I took a course in economics. I know."

"Well, then, how much to you think you need?"

"I guess it depends on how well we are planning on living."

"And?"

"And we can't quite figure it out. We don't agree."

"I am glad I don't have to hear you argue."

"Well, we don't actually argue. We pout."

"What do you mean?"

"Some nights before bed we get to discussing the future and Louise tells me how much she would enjoy living about five thousand feet up in the mountains in a little cabin, next to a fishing stream. She loved fishing as a kid, and we are never able to …"

"That's what Louise wants. And where do you figure on retiring?"

"I want to move from Nebraska to New York City. That's where things are going on. Don't need a car there. Cabs and the subway take you wherever you want to go. A car can be nuisance."

"That would save money. But can you fish in Central Park?"

Louise, sitting patiently so far, believes this conversation is getting out of control.

Where would you take this counseling session? If you were Grandpa how would you nudge this couple in the direction of harmony? How would you help them put together a plan that would result in a happy retirement?

The problem these two are living is that they do not have the same definition of how to have fun, how to retire in a way that will bring contentment. They must sit together and agree on a result, knowing that neither one is going to find a perfect thing to do after retirement. They should find the next-best: a plan they both would enjoy. That done, they should calculate what it would take to make that thing a reality and where they would live to bring their retirement life to a good result. The One{three} demands that a desired result be in focus: a plan both agree meets both their needs.

The ability in a place has to be acted upon, to be thrusted, in a way that the planned result happens.

It does not matter how many stray elements you bring to this conversation. It is worthless to give more value to a quarter million-dollar retirement fund than a fund with only half that much money. The job of retiring happy does not require any retirement fund. Yes, you must have money when you retire, but it does not have to be in a lump sum.

This family has a deep problem. It is not their only problem. For families like this; by the way, every family is "like this," the solution to problems comes from their view of reality.

Let's apply our One{three}. What is the structure of the practice, the quality, the tendency to dissolve problems as they come? It is the deep and real, vital, conscious understanding that God is all-powerful and that God's Spirit is everywhere available. This Spirit, alive and well, is present in the life of the believer with two qualities. The Spirit is able, as Amperage is able in an electric circuit.

This ability lies latent. Just as a receptacle in the kitchen has Amps ready to be used beneath the plastic cover and those Amps will do nothing until you plug in the toaster or the table lamp, in the same way, God's Holy Spirit is determined to be available but not demanding. The load, the purpose, allows Voltage to move Amperage, allows ability to be thrust to create a result.

God determined in the creation of human beings that He would not attach strings. He is not, deliberately not, going to grab control, to apply His will or to manipulate us.

What within us is the Voltage part of this structure? It is our personal will power. When we join our willingness to involve God in every part of our lives a fresh power is ready to turn on the "light" of purpose.

Only when we allow God to be wrapped in our reverent desire to accept His energy, only then can the power (Wattage) of very real creativity, continual problem solving, be our experience.

Close the circuit. Allow, determine to allow, yourself to be at one with God's ability within you. This generates joyful living, creative results, harmony and maturity in personal, spiritual and social issues: all of them.

Thrust toward life's purpose as you depend upon direction and infinite ability from our Creator.

What's The Point?

If you are one of the typical book-tasters: one who checks the last page to see if the book is worth it? Well, yes. It is worth it. But you will enjoy it more if you turn now to page one. Leave this page for later.

Why?

The reason you need to read the pages before this is that the One{three} message will make no sense unless you learn what it means.

What that expression means is deeper even than the conversations I have shared here to try to make this idea live. The point is that everything about us, all we see around us, the tremendous Universe above us, all fits into a Universal pattern.

A purpose or plan properly thought through involves something that is given the ability to perform, to move within a place, and those three: {Place Ability Thrust} – those three – are One!

We progress when we align One{three}to get needed results. Any result also can join another set as either an ability or thrust, creating still a different Result: repeatedly, infinitely over-and-over, anywhere or everywhere.

This is a tiny perception, as tiny as a key is to vast wealth in a protective vault.

The overlying reality of where we live is found in one word. This word is found in the Bible. The same religious scholars who disdain science are for the most part unaware that this one Word contains within it the most profound content of our spiritual nature, of our understanding of God, of our confidence that our seemingly temporary lives are in fact a part of a more significant reality: one that we cannot perceive today, but One that knows all about us and One who cares about us and Who has plans for our future after this trip to Earth has been completed.

The additional overlying reality of where we live is ignored by the very scientific community that disdains any contact with faith. All the while they plumb the depths of the product of the spiritual, the results of a Power well beyond any of us, and they pretend to be finding the origins of our existence, while they disdain the Bible.

The disdain of faith, so commonly found in the pronouncements of scientists, could cause us to ignore them and to refuse to trust many of their findings. It is faith that underlies and supports countless scientific observations. The "starting point" of many scientific endeavors is an assumption, or at best a "proven" hypothesis which is possibly a misunderstanding: the product of sincere but faulty reasoning and testing. Science is riddled with faith, perhaps more faith than the level of faith found in some brands of pulpit pronouncement.

Both sets of intellectuals, many scientists and theologians, can be short-sighted. It might be well to recall that the girl named Miss Understanding needs to be wary of becoming Mrs. Theboat. Yet, many in both science and religious academia have missed the boat by foggy thinking resulting in profound misunderstanding.

The "boat-missing" academics would do well to focus upon the Bible expression: the *creative WORD*. Particle physics is the study of ever-present "wigglers," waves joined to particles that in varieties more than infinite constitute everything in our Universe. What we see in these wiggling particles is the result of the infinitely complete WORD of the Creator, a pattern of speech including more than sound, having within its infinite spread the entire electromagnetic spectrum plus all the mysteries we find within all forms of matter.

The vibrations of God's intent for our surroundings are infinite and present in the very matter enlarged by scientific microscopes. Scientists study the infinite scope of God's voice when they explore matter. The spectrum chart is the graphic evidence of God's WORD.

Albert Einstein discerned the reality of this fact without exploring the full significance of his formula $E=MC^2$. That formula has never, my research suggests, been reversed as is obviously appropriate for any Algebraic formula. That formula also tells us that Matter is equal to Energy divided by (slowed infinitely by) the square of the speed of light. $M=E/C^2$.

The speed of light is infinitely fast. The speed of light squared is an absurdity. Light and all aspects of the electromagnetic spectrum cover us at the speed of light, the infinite speed that only they are capable of attaining. What Einstein, in my opinion, was telling us is, "If you speed matter beyond its ability to be sped up, you will find the source of that matter is energy." Of course, that means all the matter we see is the product of energy.

My view of his formula is that Einstein, perhaps unwittingly, was proving that the infinite creative energy of the Universe, the elements, particles and waves we believe are the result of God's Creative Word, this energy, resides in all we see, in all that is. Matter was created by an energy beyond our comprehension: WORD. The matter we see and feel all around us is the product of the Creator's infinitely fast energy called WORD. After our Creator uttered WORD, it slowed infinitely, becoming useful and visible. Oscilloscopes disclose its infinite structure and contents.

To convey his belief to his colleagues, Einstein suggested the obverse. He suggested that if we puny humans try to build an accelerator capable of reaching an unreachable speed, that the matter we subject to that torture will become energy. The Atom Bomb was the product of scientific effort demonstrating the validity of Einstein's discovery. There was no "speed of light squared" reached in the development of that weapon. However, it worked. Einstein's formula was verified over and over in the production of one after another atomic blast.

This significant part of scientific development, however, has never to my knowledge, been seen in its obverse. The point I make here: the take-away from this book that I would like you to learn, is that this place we call Earth contains an ability in the observable particles and waves all around us. That ability came from the WORD, the creative expression of God. He wants us to know that everything we are made of -- all we see and experience -- is the result of the slowed energy of His WORD.

One DOES, in fact, contain three. Creation is the result of the Father's plan, uttered by Jesus Who is the personal Word, thrusted by the Holy Spirit.

Your life is the most important place for you to consider. When you look back on it, what result would you like to see? What ability will be motivated toward the goal you want to reach? Ideally, your result and goal should be to live in a way that God will enjoy watching your life develop. Within your day to day life, if you approach life the way you should, you will face the choices and problems of life with the determined willpower to accept God's ability, His GPS, for your decisions. That done with consistency, you will experience a pleasant joyful result.

By the way, there was another adventure. It isn't about George, but I think I should tell you what happened. Louise's mother, Matilda, dropped in one day not long ago. She had just been to see her doctor and there was trouble all over her face. Louise invited Grandpa over to have a talk.

"Matilda, good to see you again. Tell me about your doctor. Is he okay?" Grandpa tried to lighten up heavy subjects.

"Very funny," she responded. "I am not sure that I'm okay. I am thinking heavy thoughts. Life is good but I know that nobody can escape death. It really bothers me. Louis tells me that you somehow have a good view of this. I am listening."

"Listening is a good start. You have a computer, right?"

"Of course."

"What if your computer was destroyed? Maybe there was a surge and your disk was fried. Totaled. Nothing else there. Will never again start up. What would you do?"

"Do?" She had no idea where Grandpa was going with this.

"How would you do any of the work? Your emails. Your schedule. All you have stored, and its all gone. How would you operate?"

"Ha! I would start over, I guess. From scratch."

"I don't think so. You would buy a new computer, tell the tech at the store about your loss and in just a few hours that tech would download all your files from THE CLOUD. Have you ever heard about the cloud?"

"I get it! Sure! Now I know what you're talking about. Of course. I hadn't thought of that. But you're right. Problem solved. What is the cloud?"

"I don't know much about it, but it's a huge computer system. Not up in the sky: in a warehouse somewhere and those computers they use have huge storage and your files automatically go up there if you set up your computer the right way."

"Sure, I know what the cloud is." She was getting his point, partly.

"Good for you." Grandpa smiled as though he was really pleased with what he was going to say next.

"What is your point?" Matilda asked.

"The point is, do you think today's techs at Google and the other massive Internet companies are smarter that God, or maybe does God know how to do their jobs? Maybe he even knows better about how to do their jobs? Maybe He is capable of having a cloud? How about it?"

"Your question answers itself," Matilda smiled.

Grandpa looked her squarely in the eyes, radiating serious thought. "Matilda, have you ever lost somebody you respect to cremation?"

Matilda was startled. She paused. "Well, uh, yes. Why do you ask?"

"Cremation pretty well destroys the human computer, doesn't it?"

"Again, you have asked a question that answers itself. So?"

"Well, if we are relating in life with the Creator the way the Bible tells us is the way to assure eternal life, doesn't it seem obvious that God has uploaded our data to His cloud, and that it will be available for whatever body we are given in Heaven? Does that thought make you feel a little more confident about anything the doctor might tell you?"

"More confident? Oh, oh, oh. I would say more content, more happy, more full of joy. Where did you get that thought?"

Grandpa smiled.

"I think I can guess. It just came to you. Right?" The elderly lady guessed.

"Yep. Your question just answered itself."

If you understand the One{three}, as Grandpa does, you know that it patterns who God is. He is Three in One: Father, Son and Holy Spirit. His pattern, his image, is everywhere. In electricity we see a vivid example, one open for examination. The One Godhead like Wattage, has within the Son, Jesus, like Amperage, driven by willpower, Voltage, like the Holy Spirit, within the Father, like your life: the place you live. That is One{three}.

Live it! Flip the switch.

You can write your thoughts on this subject to richardpalquist@gmail.com.

Let me know how you would fix George's problem with Sally. How would you apply One{three}?

About The Author

Richard Palmquist, born July 1931, earned his B.A. in 1953, from Carthage College, then-Carthage, Illinois. Married to Dolores Mae Lund that year, he went on to a three-year education in theology. The couple's fifty-seven-year marriage brought to them the joy of three sons and two daughters plus two dozen grandchildren and about a dozen great grandchildren. Dolores died in 2014.

His career in radio began in Oakland, California in 1957. He negotiated the purchase of 50kw KEAR, San Francisco, California. That purchase grew to a network of over 50 radio stations.

He spent seven years to develop Family Stations, Inc., by then a network of five radio stations, including a powerful FM station covering New York City. He went on to a brief career consulting with clients to help them earn FM station construction permits from the Federal Communications Commission.

Palmquist disdains the memory of the notorious promotion of "end of world" reports by Family Radio in 2011, fostered by Harold Camping, Palmquist's successor at Family Stations, Inc.

From 1970, until retirement in 1997, he presided over the corporation that owned KDNO, Delano, California. He and his wife, developed the Handi-Directory telephone directory and the once-weekly newspaper the ENTERPRISE NEWS, based in southern Tulare County, California.

He authored the 2005 book EINSTEIN, MONEY AND CONTENTMENT and the 2016 book, INTIMACY, GATEWAY TO HELL OR TO GOOD HEALTH, then WHAT ON EARTH ARE YOU IN HEAVEN'S NAME plus CREATIVE CONFUSION. This book is his fifth work.

Spiritual counselors encourage seekers, "allow God to use you." Though this advice is well-intentioned, the Author suggests it is not quite Biblical. In the Garden of Eden, God began His adventure with mankind by requiring responsibility. The Creator did not tell Adam "I am going to use you as a tool so I can 'take dominion.'"

No! Adam was commanded to do it himself. "Take dominion!" was the command from the Creator. This responsibility, implanted in human beings, means that we are personally like One{three}. Just as electricity uses Volts to move the ability of Amperage, God wants people to be movers, using His ability. We have been given the liberty to move-at-will. To be effective, we must take seriously our jobs while recognizing that we do not know the first thing about where we are headed. That wisdom is available to anyone who has the Holy Spirit alive inside and working, not dormant. God gives wisdom only to those who ask, just as a GPS does good only while not stored in the glove box.

The author, while writing this book, discovered a vital intimate relationship with the Holy Spirit. Instead of "Here I am: use me," he has learned that we are to be dynamic, effective, thrusters. We must cause creative things to happen. As concerned persons, we must realize how privileged we are to be confident we can set goals, find joy and fit into God's destiny for us as we seize the challenges of life.

Rightly related to God, we are in the Voltage role. In humility we see it is the infinite Holy Spirit who gives us our GPS-like ability, the lefts and right turns, as we get done the jobs life gives.

Since 1997, when he became "retarded," the author slowed down, has tried to be creative in Nipomo, California. His email address is richardpalmquist@gmail.com.

Details of his work can be found at www.richardhpalmquist.com or www.richardpalmquist.com.

www.ingramcontent.com/pod-product-compliance
Lightning Source LLC
LaVergne TN
LVHW041543060526
838200LV00037B/1111